5.95

Gilles Gauthier

A Gift from Mooch

Illustrated by Pierre-André Derome
Translated by Sarah Cummins

First Novels

D1262250

Formac Publishing Company Limited
Halifax, Nova Scotia

Formac Publishing Company Limited acknowledges the support
of the Cultural Affairs Section, Nova Scotia Department of
Tourism and Culture. We acknowledge the financial support of
the Government of Canada through the Book Publishing Industry
Development Program (BPIDP) for our publishing activities.
We acknowledge the support of the Canada Council for the Arts
for our publishing program.

National Library of Canada Cataloguing in Publication Data
Gauthier, Gilles, 1943-
[Pas de prison pour Chausson. English]
A gift from Mooch
    (First novels : #39)
    Translation of: Pas de prison pour Chausson.
    ISBN 0-88780-549-3 (bound).
    ISBN 0-88780-548-5 (pbk.)

I. Derome, Pierre-André, 1952- II. Cummins, Sarah
III. Title. IV. Series.
PS8563.A858P3813 2001   jC843'.54   C2001-902565-3
PZ7.G23436Gi 2001

Formac Publishing
Company Limited
5502 Atlantic Street
Halifax, NS B3H 1G4
www.formac.ca

JUN 2 7 2002

Printed and bound in Canada

Distributed in the U.S. by
Orca Book Publishers
P.O. Box 468 Custer, WA
U.S.A. 98240-0468

Distributed in the U.K. by
Roundabout Books (a division
of Roundhouse Publishing Ltd.)
31 Oakdale Glen, Harrogate,
N. Yorkshire, HG1 2JY

Table of Contents

1
Share a Dumpling?

Oh no! Here we go again. Can't we just have fun anymore?

"Gary, what's with you this last week? You keep hitting Dumpling for no reason, you're always shouting at me—"

"I do not shout at you!"

"Yeah, right. As soon as you walk through the door, an argument starts. You always want to have Dumpling with you. It's like you're jealous."

"Well, Dumpling *is* my dog!"

"And it's not my fault that Dumpling wants to be with me! He follows me every-where. I think he's adopted me."

"You're trying to take him away from me."

"What?"

"I'm not blind, you know. I see your little tricks. How you pet him whenever my back is turned. You wish you had Dumpling all to yourself."

"Are you out of your mind, Gary? I wish you wouldn't keep coming over after school. I want to work on my biography of Mooch. But every single day you come over and bring Dumpling!"

"After Mooch died, you were pretty glad we were around!"

"I still am. Except—"

"Except now, we have to make an appointment! We can only come by when you deign to see us. And then you do your best to steal my dog away!"

"Dumpling is like a magnet and I'm the fridge. As soon as he walks in the door, he sticks to me and he won't let go."

"You try to make him come to you and stick."

"Do you think I keep doggie bones hidden in my pockets, or what?"

"It's easy to make an animal love you. You don't have to be a rocket scientist. But remember one thing. Dumpling belongs to me. He's my dog, and no one's going to take him away from me."

"I can do without your Dumpling, if you must know. I have hundreds of pages to write about Mooch. It will keep me busy all winter long."

"Great! Just write your masterpiece, and leave my dog alone."

"Well, you can stay at your own house from now on, if you're so worried."

"You'll be sorry you said that!"

"You can shut Dumpling up in a cage and put a big lock on the door. Then no one will be able to take *your* dog away from you!"

Gary's face turned as red as a chili pepper. He grabbed

Dumpling, pushed me onto the bed, and ran out of the room, slamming the door behind him.

He had really lost it.

2
A Special Friendship

I had never had such a good friend as Gary, and I didn't want to lose him.

Once he had been my worst enemy. When I first knew him at school, he was not very nice. He was always making fun of me and my old dog Mooch.

He called me "The Klutz" because I was so bad at hockey. He called Mooch "The Skunk" because she was always getting sprayed by those stinky little pests.

Then Gary found out that

my dad had died a long time ago in a car accident. He reached out to Mooch and me and he became my best friend.

Gary often showed me how important I was for him, too.

He told me that his father, Jack, had spent four years in prison. That was a secret that he had kept from everyone

else at school.

When Mooch died, Gary wanted to give me Dumpling, even though his dad had just bought the puppy for him. He would do that just to make me feel better.

That was why I couldn't understand why Gary was acting this way.

But, Gary was my friend, and I wasn't going to let that change. I thought of a good way of showing him how important he was to me.

I would write about him in my biography of Mooch. I wouldn't dwell on the time when he wasn't very nice. But I would write pages and pages about what he did for Mooch and me.

On many occasions, Gary had helped me to track down Mooch, who was always getting lost. And Jack and Gary had come with my mom to rescue Mooch from the dog pound.

When Gary saw what I was writing, he'd know how much I cared about him.

3
Gary's Sorrow

Gary didn't show up during the week. When Jack stopped by to chat with my mom, Gary took Dumpling to his aunt's house.

On Monday, Jack told me that Gary had a lot of homework. I figured that meant Gary hadn't told Jack about our quarrel.

Over the next few days, I heard that Gary was studying for a big test. Jack was in fact surprised at how industrious Gary had become.

By Friday, Jack was getting

suspicious. He was beginning to wonder about Gary's excuses. He asked me if we had quarrelled.

I didn't know what to say. I was afraid he would think I was making it up, if I said Gary didn't want me to touch his dog any more.

"Well," I said finally, "Gary's changed. It might seem funny to you, but I think he's jealous."

Jack raised his eyebrows in surprise. I tried to explain.

"Gary seems to think that I'm trying to steal Dumpling away from him."

Jack was silent. He glanced at Judy, then he patted my head.

"I'll talk to Gary when I get

home," he said. "He'll be back here tomorrow."

Well, Saturday came, and still no Gary. But Jack thought he'd figured out what was really bothering him.

Gary was not really jealous of me and Dumpling. Instead, he was worried about Judy.

Gary never knew his own mother; she died when he was born. When Gary saw that Jack was getting closer to Judy, it was like reopening an old wound. He reacted badly.

"I know what my boy is like," said Jack. "He's like me. When I was unhappy, I tended to use my fists too. Gary had to deal with his unhappiness alone for so many years.

"When I got out of prison, I wanted to make it up to him, but I didn't know how. I couldn't say what I felt, so I bought him Dumpling. I used a poor little puppy to tell my son how much I love him."

4
Jack's Sorrow

For two weeks, I played alone after school. Even Jack didn't come by our house the second week. I was beginning to get really bored. And I noticed that Judy seemed a bit distracted.

I had a feeling she was thinking over everything that had happened. She must have been bothered by Gary's reaction. Maybe she wondered whether it was a good idea to get involved with Jack.

In the meantime, I kept busy working on my book

about Mooch. I'd already written five versions of the part about Gary.

From the kitchen, Judy watched me work. She was probably amazed at the pile of crumpled-up paper in my wastepaper basket. I never wrote so many drafts of my schoolwork.

Finally, she came over to encourage me.

"Mooch giving you a hard time?" she asked.

"It's not Mooch, it's me. I'm the author, but I can't find the right words."

"Some situations are not easy to describe."

"No matter how hard I think, whatever I write sounds so ordinary."

"Probably you want to express something very important. You want to get it just right."

"Yes, exactly."

Judy moved away, but then she came back.

"You must have wondered why Jack was sent to prison."

I dropped my pencil. I had asked myself that question a hundred thousand times. But I had never dared to ask Gary.

"If Gary wants me to know," I stammered, "he'll tell me."

"Well, Jack wants me to tell you about it. He felt awkward raising the subject himself."

Judy sat down on my bed and took my hands in hers.

"Jack seems like a very

strong man. But when his wife died, everything fell apart for him. He didn't know what to do, all alone with a tiny baby. He was so unhappy that he just wanted to forget everything."

Judy hesitated a moment before continuing.

"Jack drank too much, he got into a fight, and he seriously injured another man. He served his punishment, for four long years. Now that he's out of jail, he wants Gary to be free too. He wants to liberate Gary from all his hidden sorrows."

5
The Return of Dumpling

Gary was back! He just walked into the backyard.

Dumpling was all excited. He kept leaping around me, as if he had springs on his feet and had just fallen from the twelfth floor of an apartment building. He was crazy!

I didn't really like all that enthusiasm. I was afraid so much attention would make Gary jealous again, and he'd up and leave with his dog.

But no. I was worried for nothing. Gary liked Dumpling's antics. It made it easier for him to come back into my life.

He seemed a little ill at ease at first. He didn't say much—just asked me what I wanted to play. I suggested Frisbee. That set him talking.

"I'm so happy to be here! I was bored at my aunt's house."

"I'm happy too. You have no idea!"

"My aunt doesn't really like dogs. Dumpling was bored too. He likes to move around."

"No kidding!"

Gary laughed, then fell silent. We tossed the Frisbee back and forth a couple of times. Dumpling tried to catch it, and it hit him on the nose.

"I've written quite a lot of my biography of Mooch," I mentioned. "Yesterday I finished a chapter that has a lot about you in it."

"Me?"

"Well, it's obvious that you figure in the story of Mooch. Would you like me to read you that part?"

"You don't have to."

"I'd like to."

We ran up to my room and I got out my chapters.

Dumpling settled onto Gary's lap and perked up his ears. They were ready to hear me read.

I was as nervous as if I were going on stage. My legs were shaking as I sat down. I cleared my throat and began.

"This is the story of what happened last spring, when you offered to give me Dumpling to replace Mooch. It was a big decision for me. My chapter is called:

A Dog to Share

When Gary came by to find out what I had decided, a funny thing happened.

Instead of speaking, I ran to Gary and hugged him. Just like that. I hadn't thought about it beforehand.

I knew what Dumpling meant to Gary. I hugged him to show him that I appreciated what he had offered to do for me.

Both of us cried a little. Of course, I cry all the time, so that's not surprising. But that was the first time that I had seen Gary cry.

When we stopped crying, I told Gary what I thought. Dumpling was his dog. He shouldn't give Dumpling to me. But I was willing to help him bring Dumpling up.

I looked up from the page to see how Gary was reacting.

Two little rivulets of tears were flowing down his round, smiling cheeks.

6
An Unexpected Meeting

Gary seemed strange when he stopped by the next time. He was wearing an enormous backpack.

"Don't tell me you have too much homework to play?" I asked him right away.

He didn't answer. He started pulling me upstairs by my sleeve.

"Didn't you finish your homework?" Jack, who had driven him over, was also puzzled.

We disappeared into my room. Gary shut the door and

Dumpling climbed up onto my bed.

"What's going on?" I asked.

Gary didn't say a thing. A small smile hovered around his lips as he rummaged in the backpack.

Dumpling's tail was wagging eagerly as he tried to see what was in the bag. I was getting impatient. Gary took a spiral-bound book out of the bag.

"Do you write things too?"

Gary shook his head and handed me the book.

"I want to introduce you to my mother," he said, his voice cracking a little.

I froze. I looked at the album I was holding and didn't dare make another move. Gary

was inviting me into the heart of his life.

"You can open it. You'll see how beautiful she was."

I obeyed mechanically. On the first page was the photograph of a woman dressed in white.

"That was taken on her wedding day."

Gary was staring at the picture over my shoulder. His eyes were filled with tears.

I was moved too. It felt as if a thick fog had enveloped us. When I spoke, my voice felt thick too.

"I'm sure I would have loved her."

7
A Time for Tears

When we came out of my room, Jack and Judy were in the kitchen. Mom must have made a joke, because Jack was roaring with laughter.

His laughter stopped abruptly when he saw the album in his son's hands.

Gary tried to smile and took the bull by the horns.

"I wanted Carl to know about my mother. He's my best friend, after all."

Jack just stared at Gary. He seem dumbfounded by

what Gary had done. I tried to help out.

"I told Gary about my dad too, and I showed him some pictures."

I glanced at Judy. She seemed touched.

Jack continued to stare at his son. His eyes glistened with tears. Finally he lowered his eyes.

Gary walked over to his father and held out the album.

"Of course I wanted to tell Carl about my mother, because Carl talks about me in his book. He should know the real story of my life."

Jack took the album awkwardly and clutched it to his chest. Judy went to Gary and put her arm around him.

"I'm sure your dad thinks that you did the right thing."

Gary stood by Jack without moving. He seemed disconcerted by his father's tears. There was a long silence.

Slowly Jack raised his head. He seemed to want to speak, but his words were drowned by sobs.

Then Gary spoke to him, in a soft murmuring voice I had never heard before.

"Don't cry, Dad. I'm here, Dad, and I love you. Don't cry anymore."

8
A Strange Anniversary

Today is Gary's birthday. It's also the anniversary of his mother's death. For Gary, it's as if life and death are always mixed up together.

Gary is usually quite reserved, but yesterday he talked a lot. There were so many things he wanted to tell me.

"Every year when my birthday comes around, I'm scared. Everyone else looks forward to their birthday, but not me. It brings back too many bad memories.

"My mother died giving birth to me. My father went away when I was five years old. When I started school, I really understood what I was missing.

"Instead of saying 'my mom,' I had to say 'my aunt.' And I didn't have much chance to say 'dad.'

"I was supposed to have a father, but I didn't see him very often. Before he went to jail, he used to drink a lot. Afterwards, I had to tell lies.

"You remember how I used to pretend that my dad was taking a trip around the world. I was always afraid my secret would be found out and people would know that wasn't true.

"So I tried to prevent that. I did whatever I needed to do so that people would leave me alone. If anyone got curious, I punched them in the nose.

"Then one day, there was you, and your old dog Mooch. Then later, there was my father again, and Dumpling.

"I was so happy that I finally had my own father and my own dog. I didn't believe it could last. Every night I would say to myself, 'Something is bound to happen.'

"Then Dumpling started to get attached to you, and my dad started to get attached to Judy. I was afraid. I was afraid I would lose what I had only had for such a short time."

I tried to tell Gary it was all right. Dumpling was his dog, and no one would take him away. Judy was not going to steal his father. Jack was going to stay with him for good.

Today, Gary will see that all this is true.

Gary has never gone with his father to visit his mother's grave. In fact, Jack hasn't been to the cemetery at all since he got out of jail.

Mom explained to me that Jack still felt too guilty. He couldn't forgive himself for abandoning Gary.

But today, it will be different. Jack will go to the cemetery with Gary, and together they'll put flowers on the grave.

When they come back, we'll have a party here. Judy has already made a three-layer chocolate cake. And I am planning a very special present for my friend.

I have unlocked the chest where I keep my souvenirs of Mooch. I am going to give Gary the one souvenir that I hold dearest.

9
A Day to Remember

When Gary and Jack got out of the car, they looked like long-lost lovers. Gary had his arm around his dad's waist and, although their eyes were red, they were both smiling.

They were ready for the party!

Gary ate like there was no tomorrow, scarfing down four slices of cake. Dumpling probably ate just as much. He had chocolate up to his ears.

Then Gary unwrapped his present from me. I hid it inside five different boxes,

to make the suspense last
longer. Finally he got to the
fifth box.

"I wonder what it can be!"

"You'll find out in a
second."

Gary lifted the lid of the
box and his face lit up.

"Wow! The Rocket Richard
hockey jersey that your dad
got you! Number 9 on the

Canadiens! Are you sure you want to give this to me?"

"I thought you might like it."

"It's the best present I've ever had! And you know what we can do, Carl? We can dress Dumpling in it for Halloween. He'll be disguised just like you disguised Mooch."

"It might be a bit big for Dumpling."

"It doesn't matter. We'll put my shoulder pads underneath. Dumpling will look just like a huge German shepherd."

Everyone burst out laughing, except Dumpling. He kept sniffing the sweater. Maybe he was worried that Mooch was still around somewhere.

"Don't worry, little Dumpling. Old Mooch won't mind if you wear the sweater. She would be happy to see you following in her footsteps."

Gary was staring at the sweater, but he wasn't seeing it. He was lost in thought.

"Last night I had a dream," he said. "I just now remembered it, because of the sweater. Mooch was in my dream."

This startled me, and I was curious.

"What was my dog doing in your dream?"

"In the beginning, she wasn't in the dream. I was at the pound, and I saw Dumpling there. He was locked up in a big cage, like Mooch was that time. Dumpling looked desperate."

"Then what happened?"

"Then, everyone came— Jack, Judy, you, and me. My dad opened the cage."

"Are you sure this was a dream? It sure sounds like what already happened."

"Wait, I haven't finished yet. When the door was

opened, Dumpling didn't move right away. He kept looking up into the sky, as if he was hypnotised.

"Then we all looked up into the sky and just stood there, staring in amazement.

"On a cloud above Dumpling's head stood my mother, your father, and Mooch, all smiling at us."

Meet all the great kids in the *First Novels Series*!

Meet Arthur—an only child with a great Dad

- *Arthur Throws a Tantrum*
- *Arthur's Dad*
- *Arthur's Problem Puppy*

Meet Carrie—who is determined to try new things, no matter the results

- *Carrie's Crowd*
- *Go For It, Carrie*
- *Carrie's Camping Adventure*

Meet Duff—always on the lookout for adventure

- *Duff's Monkey Business*
- *Duff the Giant Killer*

Meet Fred—whose wild imagination and love of cats gets him into all kinds of trouble!

- *Fred on the Ice Floes*
- *Fred and the Food*
- *Fred and the Stinky Cheese*
- *Fred's Dream Cat*
- *Fred's Midnight Prowler*

Meet Jan—resourceful Jan, whose persistence sometimes goes too far

- *Jan's Awesome Party*
- *Jan on the Trail*
- *Jan and Patch*
- *Jan's Big Bang*

Meet Lilly—who likes to play with her friends and help out in her neighbourhood

- *Lilly's Good Deed*
- *Lilly Plays her Part*
- *Lilly to the Rescue*

Meet the Loonies—pocket-size people who like to have fun

- *Loonie Summer*
- *The Loonies Arrive*

Meet Maddie— irrepressible Maddie whose family is just too much sometimes

- *Maddie Needs her Own Life*
- *Maddie in Trouble*
- *Maddie Goes to Paris*
- *Maddie in Danger*
- *Maddie in Goal*
- *Maddie Tries to Be Good*
- *Maddie Wants Music*
- *Maddie Wants New Clothes*
- *That's Enough Maddie!*

Meet Marilou—and her clan of clever friends

- *Marilou, Iguana Hunter*
- *Marilou on Stage*
- *Marilou's Long Nose*

Meet Mikey—a small boy with a big problem

- *Mikey Mite's Best Present*
- *Good For You, Mikey Mite!*
- *Mikey Mite Goes to School*
- *Mikey Mite's Big Problem*

Meet Mooch—and Carl, who is learning lessons about life thanks to his dog Mooch

- *A Gift from Mooch*
- *Missing Mooch*
- *Mooch Forever*
- *Hang On, Mooch!*
- *Mooch Gets Jealous*
- *Mooch and Me*
- *Life without Mooch*

Meet Morgan—who always seems to be in the right place at the wrong time

- *Great Play, Morgan*
- *Morgan's Secret*
- *Morgan and the Money*
- *Morgan Makes Magic*
- *Great Play, Morgan*

Meet Robyn—an only child who is looking for ways to have more fun

- *Robyn's Best Idea*
- *Robyn Looks for Bears*
- *Robyn's Want Ad*
- *Shoot for the Moon, Robyn*

Meet the Swank Twins—who do everything together

- *The Swank Prank*
- *Swank Talk*

Meet other First Novel friends

- *Leo and Julio*
- *Max the Superhero*
- *Will and His World*
- *Video Rivals*

Formac Publishing Company Limited
5502 Atlantic Street,
Halifax, Nova Scotia
B3H 1G4
www.formac.ca
Orders: 1-800-565-1975
Fax: (902) 425-0166